THE RACE OF THE GOLDEN APPLES

THE RACE OF THE GOLDEN APPLES

by CLAIRE MARTIN
illustrated by LEO and DIANE DILLON

DIAL BOOKS FOR YOUNG READERS
NEW YORK

Published by Dial Books for Young Readers
A Division of Penguin Books USA Inc.
375 Hudson Street
New York, New York 10014

Text copyright © 1991 by Claire Martin
Illustrations copyright © 1991 by Leo and Diane Dillon
Printed in the USA
First Edition
10 9 8 7 6 5 4 3 2 1

Library of Congress Cataloging in Publication Data

Martin, Claire.
The race of the golden apples.

Summary: A Greek princess, raised by bears in the forest
and then returned to her rightful place in the kingdom,
refuses to marry unless the man can outrun her in a footrace.
1. Atalanta (Greek mythology)—Juvenile literature.
[1. Atalanta (Greek mythology.)   2. Mythology, Greek.]
I. Dillon, Leo, ill.   II. Dillon, Diane, ill.
III. Title.
JUV BL820.A835M37 1991   292'.13 [E]   85-16290
ISBN 0-8037-0248-5
ISBN 0-8037-0249-3 (lib. bdg.)

The full-color paintings were created using acrylics on acetate.
The borders are pastel on bristol board. The artwork was scanner-separated
and reproduced as red, blue, yellow, and black halftones.

To Chet, who runs the good race,
and to Richard and Philip, whose races are run

C.M.

To Lee

L.D. and D.D.

Wolves pricked up their ears. A faint cry reached them, carried on the night breeze. The wolf leaders sniffed the air, catching a hated scent. Silently the pack loped toward the cry, the moon glinting in their yellow eyes.

They found a baby, alone on the mountain. Warily they circled closer.

Half hidden by the trees, two figures were watching. One, tall and stately, dressed like a hunter, held a bow taut. By her side a shaggy, awkward she-bear was still yawning from sleep.

Suddenly the huge leader of the wolves snarled and darted toward the child. The huntress raised her bow and let the arrow fly. The wolf yelped once, twisted in the air, and fell dead beside the crying baby.

Diana, the Goddess of the Hunt, stepped into the clearing. She urged Crona, the she-bear, forward until the bear lumbered over to the howling infant. Crona nursed the baby and kept her warm, mothering her as her own cub.

The girl grew to be tall, strong, and full of laughter. Her playmates were the forest animals. She delighted to swim swift-flowing rivers and ran like the wind. Racing against the nimble stag, she would easily outrun him.

Diana's nymphs loved the pretty human child. They braided her fair hair with bright woodland flowers and taught her the language and customs of people. Diana herself gave the girl an ivory hunting bow and arrows, and trained her to use them. Soon her skill rivaled the Goddess's.

One day Diana gently told the child of that night on the mountain long ago. She learned that her father was the violent ruler, King Iasus. He had been angry that his firstborn was not a son and had ordered the baby to be abandoned.

"But," Diana said, "that night Crona and I saved you. Your name is Atalanta, and you are a princess of Greece."

The girl stared at the Goddess and her face grew pale. Finally she spoke. "I suppose I'm lucky then. I live in the forest instead of a castle. And I don't have to know a father who is so cruel!" Diana nodded, but her glance was tinged with sadness.

On a crisp fall day a young hunter was walking quietly in the forest when he came upon Atalanta wrestling with her foster brother, Obrin. To the hunter it looked as though a savage bear were attacking a helpless child. He ran forward and plunged his sword deep into the bear's side. Then, shaken, he turned to see if the girl was all right. Blue eyes blazed at him above an arrow aimed straight at his heart.

"Atalanta, don't!" Diana's voice rang through the glade, shaking the leaves of the trees. But the angry girl shot the arrow anyway. Diana appeared suddenly between Atalanta and the hunter, knocking the arrow aside. It fell harmlessly on the grass.

"Go! Leave us!" Diana ordered the young man. Fearing the Goddess's anger, he quickly obeyed. Then she faced the girl. "You dare to disobey me?" she demanded.

"I'm sorry, Goddess," Atalanta cried, "but he killed Obrin!" She fell at Diana's feet. "You can save him . . . can't you?" she begged.

"I cannot. He belongs to Death now."

Atalanta's eyes brimmed over with tears. "Then why did you stop me from avenging my brother's death?" she implored.

Her grief softened Diana's anger. "The boy was blameless. He only tried to help you," she replied.

"I hate the human race," Atalanta cried bitterly. "They bring nothing but pain and death." An icy coldness filled her heart. She dried her tears, but her eyes glinted like frozen mountain ponds.

"Never forget, Atalanta, they are your people. Soon it will be time for you to take your place in your father's kingdom."

"No, Goddess! Never!" answered the girl. "I will always live here in the woods. *This* is my kingdom. How could you want me to return to a father who tried to kill me?"

"King Iasus regrets his cruelty toward you. He is old now and longs for an heir." The Goddess placed her hands on the girl's shoulders and looked into her eyes. "It is your destiny, Atalanta. You must go. You defied me once. Do not do so again. The gods will be obeyed!"

As Atalanta strode toward the castle, the townspeople stared at the beautiful girl in the forest-green tunic, who neither looked at them nor smiled. Her father greeted her and embraced her. But Atalanta's arms stayed stiff at her sides, her hands clenched.

During the years Atalanta lived at court, she always longed for her home in the forest. She watched her father rule with a strong, harsh

will. She learned from him how to be cruel. Anyone who tried to show her love and kindness she turned coldly aside.

Years passed, and King Iasus wanted Atalanta to marry. Many noblemen courted her, but though her father insisted she choose one, Atalanta scorned them all. Finally the King decided on a contest. Whoever proved to be the strongest would win Atalanta for his wife.

Atalanta was furious. "What does it matter to me if one of these weak men can triumph over the others?" she exclaimed. "None of them — no man alive — is my equal. No one has ever outrun me in a footrace!"

"If there were one," the King asked quickly, "would you consent to marry him?"

Atalanta knew her speed could not be matched. She agreed.

"So be it, then," the King declared. "But for such a great prize, there must be a great penalty. What must they give up if they fail?"

Looking steadily at the King, Atalanta replied, "They must give up their lives."

The day of the race dawned hot and clear. The hero Hippomenes was the appointed judge. Not only was he descended from the gods, but he had also won honor for his many courageous deeds. When he was scarcely more than a boy, he was said to have slain a ferocious bear.

As Hippomenes watched the dozens of eager young men gather, he thought, how foolish they are to risk their lives to win a wife.

Just then Atalanta appeared, proud and tall, in a light-blue tunic that fluttered with the breeze. Hippomenes was stunned. This was the girl he had seen years before in the forest. He remembered her angry eyes flashing when she leveled her bow at him. He remembered the pain he had caused her. Suddenly he knew that he had loved her since he first saw her. He knew that he would be glad to die for her. He looked again at the young men, fearing that one of them might win.

The trumpets sounded the start of the race. Atalanta dashed forward like an arrow shot from her ivory bow. Moving with the speed and grace of a splendid bird in flight, she easily outdistanced all the young men. Then she turned away, as they were led to their deaths.

At last Hippomenes stepped forward. "Princess," he said, "you once desired my death because I killed a bear you loved. Here is your chance — race against me!"

Atalanta looked at the strong, handsome man before her, and a feeling of pity stirred inside her. "Yes, Hippomenes, I remember you. But I know now that you tried to save me in the forest. Please do not challenge me, for you cannot win."

"I have no choice. You see," he added with a smile, "I am in love with you and cannot live without you."

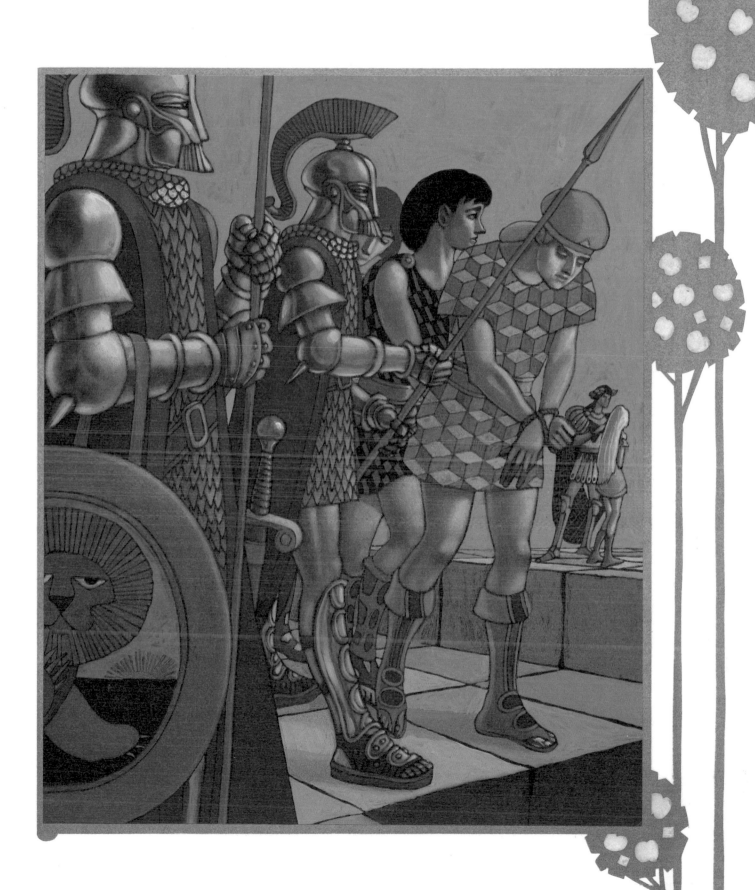

Atalanta tried to prepare for the race, but her thoughts whirled. Should she cause the death of this brave man who had once risked his life for her? Perhaps he would outrun her. No, he could not, she was sure. And she was determined not to marry. "Poor Hippomenes," she sighed. "I wish you had never seen me."

At the edge of the race course Hippomenes prayed to Venus, the Goddess of Love. "You who made me love," he cried, "help me now or I will die."

In her temple Venus heard the prayer. She went to her garden, where a beautiful apple tree grew with shining leaves and fruit of pure gold. Venus picked three apples and hurried to Hippomenes. Invisible to everyone else, she handed them to him and told him how to use them.

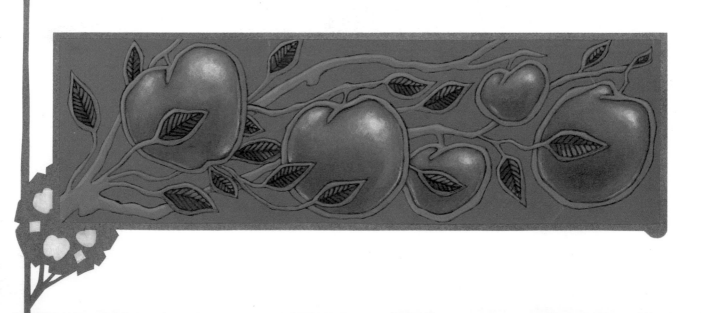

The two runners lined up for the start of the race. At the trumpets' sound both Hippomenes and Atalanta shot forward, skimming over the sand. Often, when she could have passed him, Atalanta lingered by Hippomenes' side, gazing at his graceful form. She smiled as she remembered racing with the stag in the forest. At last she pulled ahead.

Hippomenes ran faster than he ever had but could not catch her. He thought of the apples, and taking the first, he rolled it past Atalanta. The sparkling fruit immediately caught her eye and, struck by its beauty, she bent to pick it up. Seizing the opportunity, Hippomenes dashed by her, but Atalanta quickened her pace and regained the lead.

Again Hippomenes threw an apple, this time farther off the course. Quick as a swallow, the girl darted to the side, stooped to pick up the apple, and again overtook her challenger.

Hippomenes almost despaired as he saw how quickly she passed him. He was nearing the end of his strength. His breath rasped past his dry lips. Try as hard as he might, he could run no faster. Without Venus's help, he knew he must die.

Now the finish line was near. With a quick prayer to Venus, and almost the last of his strength, he hurled the third apple far off the course. Atalanta saw it gleam, then glanced at the finish line approaching. Victory could be hers. Hippomenes would lose.

Tears stung her eyes as she remembered the death of Obrin, her foster brother. But then she pictured Hippomenes being led to *his* death, and her anger vanished. She made her choice.

Atalanta veered off the course and bent down to retrieve the apple. Hippomenes raced across the finish line, the winner.

When he came to her, Atalanta was laughing for the first time since she had left her forest.